BATMAN BEGINS™

THE MOVIE STORYBOOK

Adapted by Benjamin Harper

Screenplay by Christopher Nolan and David S. Goyer
Story by David S. Goyer

Batman created by Bob Kane

SCHOLASTIC

Photos courtesy of Warner Bros.

Scholastic Children's Books
Commonwealth House, 1-19 New Oxford Street
London WC1A 1NU, UK
a division of Scholastic Ltd
London ~ New York ~ Toronto ~ Sydney ~ Auckland
Mexico City ~ New Delhi ~ Hong Kong

First published in the USA by Scholastic Inc., 2005
First published in paperback in the UK by Scholastic Ltd, 2005

© 2005 DC Comics
THE BATMAN, DC Bullet Logo, and all related characters and elements are trademarks of and © DC Comics
WB logo: TM and © Warner Bros. Entertainment Inc.

ISBN 0 439 96081 9

All rights reserved

Printed by Proost, Belgium

2 4 6 8 10 9 7 5 3 1

This book is sold subject to the condition that it shall not,
by way of trade or otherwise, be lent, resold, hired out,
or otherwise circulated without the publisher's prior consent
in any form of binding or cover other than that in which it is published
and without a similar condition, including this condition,
being imposed upon the subsequent purchaser.

"Bruce!"
Young Bruce Wayne and his friend Rachel Dawes were playing on the Wayne estate when Bruce fell into an abandoned well.

He spiralled down into the darkness and landed hard. Something rustled in the gloom. As it scuttled closer, Bruce trembled in fear.

Hundreds of angry bats swirled around Bruce as they swooped up the shaft of the well. Bruce thrashed his arms and screamed, but he could not escape the swarming bats.

Years later, Bruce woke up in a nightmare of another kind —
a jail cell deep in the heart of Asia. He had spent his youth searching
the planet to find a solution to his sadness and had wound up trapped
in a violent prison.

At breakfast several prisoners attacked Bruce, but he defeated them
all. The guards threw him into solitary confinement for protection — not
for Bruce's safety, but to protect the other inmates!

In the dark cell, Bruce was surprised to find that he was not alone.

"I thought this was supposed to be solitary confinement," he muttered.

"My name is Ducard, but I speak for Rā's al Ghūl," said a voice. "Rā's al Ghūl and his League of Shadows offer a path to those who can uphold our code."

"Code?" Bruce asked.

"This world is run by tyrants," Ducard said. "Our code respects only the natural order of things. There is a rare poppy that grows on the eastern slopes. Tomorrow you will be released. Pick one of the flowers. If you can carry it to the monastery on top of the mountain, you may find what you're looking for."

"What am I looking for?" asked Bruce.

"Purpose," Ducard replied.

B ruce pushed his way through the driving snow up an icy ridge until he finally reached an ancient monastery perched on top of a rocky outcrop. He staggered to the vast doors and pounded on them with all of his remaining strength.

There was no answer.

Frantic, Bruce pounded and pounded until he finally heard the doors grinding open. He stumbled into a massive hall. Bruce's hand trembled as he held up the blue poppy he'd found. At the far end, the dark, robed figure of Rā's al Ghūl waited, seated on a throne.

Bruce approached but was immediately surrounded by an army of ninja. They were armed and ready to attack.

"Wait," Ducard told the ninja. He was leaning against a pillar nearby.

Rā's al Ghūl spoke to Bruce, and Ducard translated. "We will help you conquer your fear. In exchange, you will renounce the cities of man. You will live in solitude. You will be a member of the League of Shadows, and you will be without fear."

Bruce's training in the League of Shadows began immediately for Ducard lunged at him even though he was exhausted.

"Death does not wait for you to be ready," shouted Ducard. "Death is not considerate or fair!"

Bruce snapped out of his fatigue and fought back. He used his previous training in ju-jitsu to fend off his attacker.

Ducard sensed something was wrong with Bruce. "You are afraid," he said, "but not of me. Tell us, Wayne, what do you fear?"

His father rushed into his bedroom. "The bats again?"

Bruce nodded.

Owner of Wayne Industries, Bruce's father was the most important man in Gotham City, but he still had time to be loving and devoted to his son. "You know why they attacked? They were afraid of you."

"Afraid of me?" asked Bruce.

"You're a lot bigger than a bat, aren't you?" his father replied comfortingly. "All creatures feel fear, even the scary ones."

Then Bruce was flooded with the memory of the night he and his parents left an opera performance early because a scene with bats had filled him with terror.

After exiting into an alley behind the theatre, the Waynes were stopped by a man holding a gun.

"Wallet, jewellery!" the man yelled. "Fast!"

Bruce's parents were obeying the man when the gun went off. Twice.

Suddenly an orphan, Bruce was left in the care of Alfred, the family butler. Bruce couldn't help blaming himself for his parents' death. "I made them leave the theatre," he cried to Alfred later.

"No, no, Master Bruce," Alfred reassured him. "Nothing you did, nothing anyone ever did can excuse that man."

Back in the Himalayan monastery, Ducard asked, "Do you still feel responsible?"

"My anger outweighs my guilt," replied Bruce.

Over the next weeks, Bruce stayed at the monastery and was trained in the ancient art of ninjutsu. He and Ducard practised their sword techniques and Ducard gave him lessons in how to defeat his enemies using any means possible.

"Theatricality and deception are powerful agents," Ducard said. "To be a great warrior is not enough. Flesh and blood, however skilled, can be destroyed. You must be more than a man in the eyes of your opponents."

To prove his point, Ducard tossed a pinch of explosive powder, creating a brilliant burst of blinding fire.

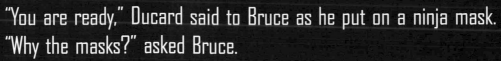

"You are ready," Ducard said to Bruce as he put on a ninja mask.

"Why the masks?" asked Bruce.

"To conquer fear," replied Ducard, "you must become fear."

All the ninja stepped towards Bruce — the nearest one slashing at him with his sword. Bruce dashed through the group, fighting for his life as each ninja continued the assault.

One by one, Bruce fought off the ninja attackers until at last he had defeated even Ducard.

"We have purged you of your fear," Ducard declared. "You are ready to lead these men." He gestured at the ninja seated around him. "As Gotham's favoured son, you will be ideally placed to help us destroy the city."

The horror of what Ducard said sank in. Bruce couldn't destroy Gotham City — it was his home! He would fight to protect it against these men.

Bruce smashed a candle to the ground, setting the monastery on fire.

"What are you doing?" cried Ducard.

"What's necessary," Bruce answered. He swiftly knocked Ducard unconscious with the hilt of his sword.

Rā's al Ghūl leapt off his throne and attacked Bruce with stunningly quick blows. As the monastery burned, Bruce battled furiously with the leader of the League of Shadows. Just when Bruce felt he might be losing the fight, a burning chunk of the ceiling fell — and crushed Rā's al Ghūl.

Bruce grabbed Ducard and dragged him safely to a small mountain village. Then Bruce left the mountain and went home to Gotham City.

Gotham was overrun by crime and violence. Bruce had to do something to stop the decay. He needed a plan.

He was walking the grounds of Wayne Manor when he came to the well he had fallen into as a child. Bruce lowered himself down the well shaft and found a crumbling crevice at the bottom.

As Bruce pushed the rocks aside, air rushed into his face. He turned on a lamp he had brought. He had discovered an immense cavern. Looking up, Bruce saw the ceiling move — it was alive! Thousands of bats swooped down and swarmed him in a cyclone.

Bruce needed a fearsome symbol to use in his fight to bring Gotham to its former glory. As he stood among the bats, he was suddenly certain what that symbol would be.

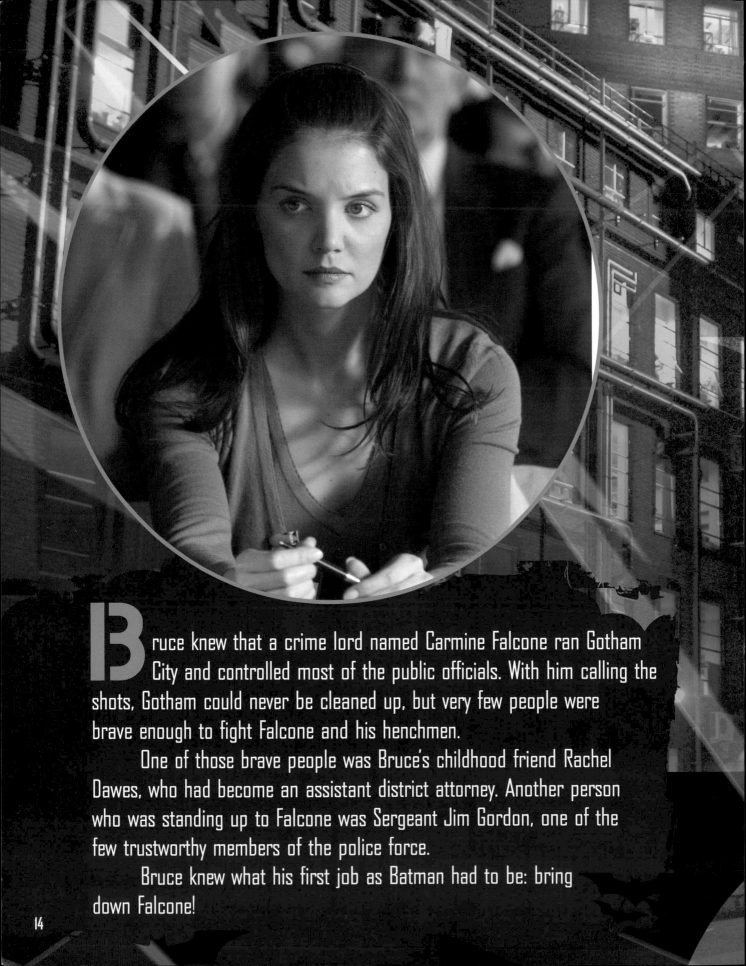

Bruce knew that a crime lord named Carmine Falcone ran Gotham City and controlled most of the public officials. With him calling the shots, Gotham could never be cleaned up, but very few people were brave enough to fight Falcone and his henchmen.

One of those brave people was Bruce's childhood friend Rachel Dawes, who had become an assistant district attorney. Another person who was standing up to Falcone was Sergeant Jim Gordon, one of the few trustworthy members of the police force.

Bruce knew what his first job as Batman had to be: bring down Falcone!

Bruce drove through the decaying streets of Gotham on his way to Wayne Industries. He had decided to work at his family's company, in the Applied Sciences division. This division created all sorts of experimental equipment for military use. Bruce wanted to get his hands on those top secret devices for his fight against Falcone.

In the Applied Sciences office, Bruce met Lucius Fox, who was in charge of the division. Out of loyalty to the Wayne family, Lucius agreed to share all sorts of devices with Bruce.

"Here it is — the Nomex survival suit for advanced infantry," Lucius said, showing Bruce a near-bulletproof, tear-resistant outfit. "This sucker will stop a knife!"

Batman was ready to make his first move. He slunk across the rooftops of Gotham City. Using ninja claws attached to his hands and feet, he scaled the wall of the police station until he entered Sergeant Gordon's office.

Gordon, busy working at his desk, didn't notice Batman until the lights went out. Startled, Gordon cried, "What do you want?"

"You're a good cop," said Batman. "One of the few. What would it take to stop Falcone?"

Gordon explained that it would be very difficult to stop the crime lord since he influenced everything in Gotham. "Who are you?" he asked.

"Watch for a sign," Batman said. Then he vanished out of the window.

Gordon ran to the window and saw Batman racing towards a gap between two office buildings. When Batman reached it, he dropped to a building below, then melted into the shadows.

Back at Wayne Industries, Lucius showed Bruce more secret weapons, including a magnetic grappling hook that could hold up to 160kg and a very impressive item called memory fabric. If the fabric was curved in a certain shape and an electrical current was run through it, the fabric would stay in place. Bruce could make lightweight wings!

Then Lucius showed Bruce the lab's most important creation — the Tumbler, a massive armoured car. As Bruce and Lucius zoomed in the Tumbler over a test track, Lucius explained its finer points. The Tumbler could jump without using a ramp!

"Does it come in black?" Bruce asked.

In the Batcave, Alfred helped Bruce perfect his Batsuit. To test Batman's mask, Alfred smashed it with a baseball bat. The mask cracked in two.

"Avoid landing on your head," advised Alfred.

Instead of replying, Bruce concentrated on grinding a piece of metal into a bat shape.

"Why the design, Master Wayne?" Alfred asked, puzzled.

"A man, however strong, is just flesh and blood," Bruce answered. "I need to be more than a man. I need to be a symbol."

"Why a bat?" asked Alfred.

"Bats once frightened me," Bruce replied. "It's time my enemies shared that dread." He hurled his finished Batarang and it whistled into the cavern's darkness.

Down at the docks, several thugs were unloading boxes. Detective Flass, Carmine Falcone and Dr Jonathan Crane, the head of Arkham Asylum, inspected the contents. The boxes contained stuffed animals filled with a mysterious substance.

"You know who we're working for," Crane told Falcone. "When he sees what's been going on, he won't be happy."

"He's coming to Gotham?" asked Falcone.

"Soon," replied Crane.

One thug near the loading dock called to his partner. No reply. He went to search for him, only to discover a giant bat hanging from a crane. The bat extended his huge wings and swooped towards the thug.

The thug screamed as he was knocked off his feet and blackness enveloped him.

The rest of Falcone's henchmen heard the scream and ran towards the loading area. They met the black shape hovering above the docks.

Falcone, anxious to find out exactly what was going on with his men, hurried into the loading area to investigate. He rounded a corner and discovered his henchmen in a circle, frightened and confused.

Into the centre of their circle dropped a black shadow that confronted the thugs, kicking them and ducking their attacks with precision. The thugs were either knocked out or ran away.

"What are you?" screamed Falcone.

"I'm Batman," the masked man replied.

Gordon and the police arrived at the docks after all of the action had finished. They found the shipment of the mysterious substance smashed up and surrounded by unconscious criminals.

"Falcone's men?" one cop asked.

"Does it matter?" Gordon replied. "We'll never tie it to him, anyway."

"I wouldn't be too sure of that," said the cop, pointing up.

Gordon looked up too. Against the night sky, the symbol of a bat shone from a searchlight. As Gordon approached the searchlight, he saw Falcone strapped to the light, arms outstretched, creating the bat's shape.

R achel Dawes beamed, tossing a newspaper onto the district attorney's desk. The front page had a huge picture of Falcone strapped to the searchlight.

"No way to bury it now," Rachel said, meaning Falcone's involvement in the crime. "Even if his partners swear in court to being thrashed by a giant bat, we have Falcone at the scene!"

Rachel was thrilled that she would be able to use her job as assistant district attorney to help Gotham battle its worst crime lord. Maybe things were finally turning around for the city!

Dr Crane was buzzed through the thick steel doors of the prison. He asked a prison guard for permission to see their newest prisoner, Carmine Falcone.

"He's probably looking for an insanity plea," said the guard, leading Crane to a holding room where Falcone was waiting.

"We've got a lot to talk about," Falcone told Crane once they were alone. "How are you going to convince me to keep my mouth shut? I know you wouldn't want the cops taking a closer look at that powder they seized. I know about your experiments on the inmates at your nuthouse. So, what was that powder I was bringing in for you, Crane?"

"If he wanted you to know," replied Crane, "he'd have told you himself."

Crane reached into his briefcase and pulled out a strange object. "Would you like to see my mask?" he asked calmly, slipping the hideous burlap sack over his head. "I use it in my experiments. Probably not frightening to a guy like you, but to those crazies . . ."

A cloud of white smoke billowed out of Crane's briefcase. "They scream and cry," Crane continued through the air filter in his mask.

As Falcone gazed at Crane, the smoke took effect. Lizard tongues flicked out of the mask. Flames spurted out of Crane's eyes and mouth. Falcone screamed in absolute horror, losing his mind.

A few minutes later, Crane emerged from the room, smiling in satisfaction. "Oh, he's not faking insanity," he told the guard. "I'll see if I can get the judge to move him to the secure wing at Arkham Asylum."

Meanwhile, Richard Earle, the head of Wayne Industries, was receiving a report about some trouble. Rogers, a senior executive, explained that one of the company's cargo ships had been found heavily damaged, and a prototype weapon had been stolen from its hold.

Earle covered his face with his hands — that was very bad news. The weapon, a microwave emitter, was designed for desert warfare. It used focused microwaves to vaporize an enemy's water supply.

"It looks like someone fired it up at sea, judging from the damage to the ship," Rogers continued.

"What about the weapon?" Earle asked.

"It's missing," Rogers said.

As Detective Flass walked down the street, he was caught — and pulled up between buildings until he was face to face with Batman. "Who was with Falcone at the docks?" Batman asked.

"I never knew his name . . . never," Flass babbled. "There was something in the powder — something hidden. I never went to the drop-off — it's in the Narrows! Cops can't go to the Narrows except in force!"

Gotham's masked defender clenched his fists. "Batman can," he said.

The Narrows, an island in the middle of Gotham River, was a decaying puzzle of public housing and makeshift buildings circling Arkham Asylum.

Batman landed on the Narrows and slipped into a warehouse. There he spied the huge industrial machine that had been stolen from the cargo ship. Standing around it were Dr Crane and several dockworkers.

Batman approached Crane and his workers — and Crane sprayed the deadly smoke in Batman's face! Batman dodged most of the poison but inhaled a little, causing him to have horrible visions.

"Need a light?" Crane threw gas and a match on Batman who toppled out of the window. On fire and fighting illusions, Batman tumbled to the ground.

He landed with a thud. The street was wet from rain, and the flames sizzled out.

"Alfred," Batman said into his mobile phone, "come quickly. I've been poisoned, and we need a blood sample."

Bruce took a sample of his blood to Lucius Fox so Lucius could concoct an antidote to the poison. He also asked Lucius to find out what the machine was that he had seen at Arkham Asylum.

"I'll make a couple of calls," Lucius said.

Bruce headed over to the district attorney's office. There he found Rachel and Sergeant Gordon discussing the case against Falcone.

"I wanted to invite you to my birthday party tonight," Bruce said to Rachel.

Before Rachel could respond, an assistant ran into her office and broke the news — Falcone had been moved to Arkham Asylum. He had gone crazy!

"Guess I won't make your party," said Rachel.

"You're not going to Arkham now!" Bruce argued. "It's in the Narrows, Rachel!"

"Happy birthday, Bruce," Rachel said, and then she raced out of her office.

Bruce knew Rachel wouldn't be safe in the Narrows. He told Alfred to keep the guests occupied at his birthday party until he returned.

"Tell that joke you knnw," he said.

Bruce stepped over to his piano, struck four notes, and waited for his secret entrance to the Batcave to swing open. He weaved down the hidden spiral staircase until he reached a dumb waiter. Climbing in, he released the lift and plummeted down into the Batcave.

When the dumb waiter hit the bottom, Bruce climbed out of it and quickly transformed himself into Batman.

At Arkham Asylum, Rachel discussed Falcone's situation with Dr Crane – she found it difficult to believe that Falcone had gone insane so quickly.

When they reached Falcone's room, Rachel peered through the window. Falcone was strapped to the bed inside, repeating the word "scarecrow" in a horrified voice.

"He's been drugged," said Rachel.

Crane told her she was correct as they continued deeper into the decrepit asylum.

Rachel replied that she didn't trust his methods and was bringing another psychiatrist out to Arkham to examine Falcone.

Crane stopped short in a room filled with vials and bags of powder. "This is where we make the medicine," he said. "Perhaps you should try some."

As he turned around, Rachel ran in the opposite direction.

Rachel tried frantically to escape the asylum, but none of the lifts were working . . . and she was lost!

"Boo."

She turned to see a hideous burlap mask and a puff of gas. Rachel fell, coughing. She screamed when she saw that the eyeholes in Crane's mask were shooting out flames.

As Crane's henchmen dragged her away, the lights in the asylum went out.

"He's here," Crane said. "The Batman. Call the police."

The thugs looked confused. "You want the *cops* here?"

"Force the Batman outside and the police will take him down."

"What about her?" the thugs asked, motioning to Rachel.

"She's gone," replied Crane. "I gave her a concentrated dose. The mind can only take so much."

Glass smashed out of a
high window as a dark
shape burst into the room.

Batman quickly roped both
of the thugs, leaving Crane hiding
somewhere with his toxic gas.

As Batman scrambled through the darkness, he could hear sirens
outside. He had to act fast! He found Rachel cowering in fear from the
awful hallucinations.

Crane burst out from the shadows, attempting to blow a cloud of
gas at Batman.

Batman grabbed Crane and ripped off his protective mask. "Taste of
your own medicine, Doctor?" he asked.

Then Batman squeezed the mask, squirting a spray of the gas right
into Crane's face.

"Who are you working for?" Batman yelled at Crane while the doctor struggled, lost in horrific visions.

"Rā's . . . al Ghūl," Crane stuttered in terror.

"Rā's al Ghūl is dead, Crane!" Batman shot back. "Who are you really working for?"

"Dr Crane isn't here right now," Crane babbled, "but if you'd like to make an appointment . . ."

Batman knew he wouldn't get any further information. He turned to Rachel, who was still writhing, battling dreadful images. Batman grabbed her and pinched a nerve, rendering her unconscious.

The police force were gathering outside. Batman had to get out of Arkham fast if he was going to get the antidote to Rachel before it was too late.

While working his way through the dark asylum, Batman ran into Sergeant Gordon.

"What happened to her?" Gordon asked, pointing at Rachel.

"Crane poisoned her with his toxin," Batman replied. "I need to give her the antidote before the damage becomes permanent. Get her downstairs and meet me in the alley on the Narrows side."

"How will you get out?" Gordon asked.

"I called for back-up. Crane's been refining his toxin, stockpiling it."

"What was he planning?"

"I don't know," said Batman, "but he's been working for someone else."

Then Batman's back-up arrived, summoned to the asylum by a sonic signal.

All of the police dived for cover as thousands of bats descended on them, swirling around their heads in a fevered whirlwind.

With a great leap, Batman dropped down the stairwell, soaring into the depths of the asylum.

Gordon dodged the bats and carried Rachel down the steps to the alley.

"Take my car," Gordon said to Batman in the alley outside the asylum.

"I brought mine," Batman said. He loaded Rachel into the Batmobile. With a loud roar, the awesome vehicle zoomed down the alley at top speed until it disappeared in the darkness.

"I've got to get one of those," Gordon muttered.

Inside the Batmobile, Batman tried to keep Rachel as calm as possible. She had regained consciousness and was struggling frantically, seeing horrible visions. It wasn't easy for Batman to concentrate on driving. A squadron of police cars was chasing him . . . along with a helicopter!

The police tailed the Batmobile as it weaved in and out of traffic, trying in vain to lose them.

Batman drove the Batmobile into a multi-storey car park, racing up to the top floor, police hot on his trail. On the roof, Batman screeched to a halt.

"Turn off your engine!" the police shouted from their vehicles.

"What are you doing?" yelled Rachel.

"Trust me," replied Batman.

Cannons shot out from the bottom of the Batmobile, blasting it over the far wall onto the roof of a nearby building. The police just stared as the Batmobile exploded from rooftop to rooftop, getting further away from them.

On the streets, the police tried to keep up with the Batmobile, which finally landed on the motorway, zooming from lane to lane, before turning off at a junction and cutting its lights on a service road.

Batman drove with night vision until he approached a waterfall. Rachel screamed as they splashed right through the waterfall . . . and landed in the Batcave.

In the Batcave, Batman rushed Rachel to a table and gave her the antidote. He then handed her a syringe and two vials, telling her to get them both to Sergeant Gordon so they could mass-produce the antidote.

Batman then gave her a sedative and promised that she would wake up soon in her own apartment. When she was sleeping, he instructed Alfred to take her home.

Then Batman changed back into his regular clothes and went to join his birthday party upstairs in Wayne Manor.

B ack at Arkham Asylum, Gordon made a grim discovery – Crane had tapped into Gotham's water supply and had been tainting it with his dangerous powder for weeks!

Gordon called a technician at the water board.

"If that's true, then it's already spread through the whole system," the technician said. "But no one's reported any effects."

"It must be like fluoride," Gordon said, "harmless to drink, but when you breathe it, it's deadly. See if there's a way to flush out the system!"

He hung up and joined a group of other officers surrounding a strange device.

"What is it?" one officer asked.

"I don't know," Gordon replied, "but nobody gets near it, understand? We're closing the bridges, locking down this whole island!"

At Bruce's party, the guests were getting ready to leave. He found Lucius and asked if he had discovered anything about the mysterious machine.

"It's a microwave emitter," Lucius whispered. "It vaporizes water."

"Could you use it to put a biological agent into the air?" Bruce asked.

"Sure," Lucius replied, "if the water supply was poisoned before it was vaporized."

Bruce was stunned. He knew what was going to happen. Then he felt a tap on his shoulder.

"Bruce, there's someone here you simply must meet," said an elderly woman, pointing to a stranger. "Now, am I pronouncing it right, Mr al Ghūl?"

"You're not Rā's al Ghūl," Bruce said, puzzled. "He's dead."

"But is Rā's al Ghūl immortal?" a familiar voice asked. "Are his methods supernatural?"

Bruce spun around and came face to face with Ducard. "Or cheap parlour tricks to conceal your true identity . . . *Rā's!*"

Ducard was actually Rā's al Ghūl!

At the asylum, the guards assigned to watch the emitter were really working for Rā's al Ghūl. After they took out the police, the ninja warriors set off an explosive and blew a huge hole through the wall.

Gordon and his men opened fire on the ninja who activated the emitter. Instantly, all the moisture boiled in the water pipes nearby. The pipes burst in explosions of pressurized steam.

As the police dived for cover, Rā's al Ghūl's henchmen escaped with the emitter.

The steam settled, leaving white clouds of poison billowing in the air. Just as Gordon disappeared into the clouds, Rachel rushed in and handed him the two vials of antidote. She repeated Batman's instructions: take one of the vials for himself and make sure the other was mass-produced to save Gotham from the effects of the poison.

"I've been admiring your handiwork even as it interfered with my plans," Rā's al Ghūl told Bruce. "You were my greatest student until you betrayed me."

Bruce spotted several members of the League of Shadows milling among the remaining guests, while Rā's al Ghūl revealed that he had hired Crane to create the poison from a substance in the blue poppies. With Gotham City destroyed, the League of Shadows would be able to take over the world!

When the last of the guests left, Rā's al Ghūl's henchmen set fire to Wayne Manor.

Rā's al Ghūl asked Bruce to return to the League of Shadows, but Bruce refused. The two fought violently as Wayne Manor burned around them. Swords clashing, they made their way through the mansion until a flaming beam landed on Bruce, knocking him unconscious.

"Rest easy, friend," Rā's al Ghūl said. Then he rushed from the burning manor to a waiting helicopter.

Wayne Manor was burning to the ground. Rā's al Ghūl had left one ninja to make sure that nobody helped Bruce.

Alfred crept up on the ninja, wielding a golf club. Just as the man turned around, Alfred whacked him on the head, knocking him out.

The beam was too heavy for the butler to move himself. Alfred slapped Bruce, waking him up, and together they pushed the beam to the side.

Flames rushed up the walls of the manor as Bruce played four notes on his piano. He and Alfred dived into the secret entrance, escaping to the safety of the Batcave.

At Arkham Asylum, Rā's al Ghūl's henchmen were loading the emitter onto a monorail train.

Below, Dr Crane — now calling himself Scarecrow — was releasing all the prisoners. Mayhem had taken over the Narrows. The dangerous prisoners had surrounded Rachel . . . and they were closing in.

Batman burst through the ring of prisoners and grabbed Rachel. Shooting his grappling gun straight up, he hoisted himself and Rachel out of the insane mob, up to one of Arkham's spires.

"They were lifting a machine up onto the tracks," Rachel reported.

"Of course!" Batman said. "The monorail — the track runs directly over the water main! He's going to drive that thing straight into Wayne Tower and blow the main hub, creating enough toxin to blanket the entire city."

Batman had to stop that train!

Rā's al Ghūl entered the conductor's carriage on the train and started it up. Three ninja henchmen guarded him and the transmitter.

As the monorail lurched into motion, Gordon, who was standing below, stood in awe as manhole covers blew off and released huge geysers of poison-filled steam.

Activating his wings, Batman glided down to the monorail, avoiding the huge jets of steam that erupted as the train passed water mains. Narrowly missing a tunnel opening, he rolled to a safe landing on the train's roof.

Rā's al Ghūl's henchmen fired at Batman, jarring him from the roof. He plummeted from the train but managed to latch his grappling hook onto it. Hanging fifteen feet below, Batman was dragged along as the monorail jetted towards Wayne Tower.

A truck filled with Rā's al Ghūl's henchmen followed below and fired grenades. Straining, Batman swung out of firing range and managed to drag himself up to the train's rear carriage.

After jumping into the carriage, Batman downed a ninja by firing his grappling gun at his feet. Then he smashed his way through the monorail until he was finally face to face with Rā's al Ghūl just as Wayne Tower appeared through the windshield.

"You!" Rā's al Ghūl screamed. He drew his sword and leapt at Batman, who dodged the blow.

The two fought mercilessly until Rā's al Ghūl knocked Batman down. Rā's al Ghūl swung the final stroke but was astonished when Batman caught the sword between his steel gauntlets. The sword snapped in two.

Rā's al Ghūl stumbled backwards, and Batman threw his grappling gun into the guiding wheel of the monorail, bumping it off its track.

"What are you doing?" Rā's al Ghūl shouted.

"What's necessary," Batman replied.

Rā's al Ghūl dived onto Batman and began to choke him as the train plummeted off its tracks. "Are you afraid?" he asked.

"Yes," Batman said, "but not of you." He activated his wings, broke free of Rā's al Ghūl's hold, and leapt from the train.

Batman glided to safety as the monorail, the emitter, Rā's al Ghūl and his fiendish plot to destroy Gotham City all plummeted into the street below and smashed into a cloud of dust and debris.

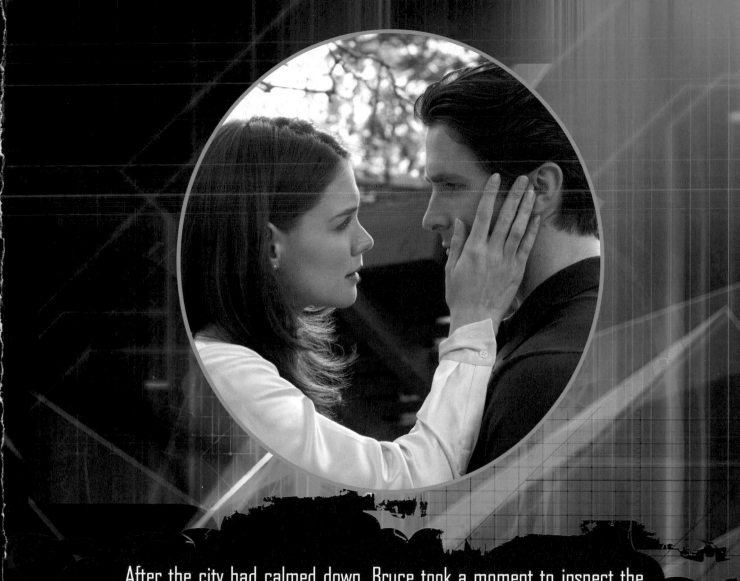

After the city had calmed down, Bruce took a moment to inspect the smoking ruin that had been Wayne Manor. Rachel found him placing boards over the entrance to the old well.

"Do you remember the day I fell?" Bruce asked.

"Of course," Rachel replied.

"As I lay down there, I sensed that things would never be the same." Rachel cocked her head curiously. "What did you find down there?"

Bruce picked up a board. "Childhood's end," he replied. "Now I see that justice is about more than my own pain and anger."

"Your father would be proud of you," Rachel said softly. "Just as I am." She looked up at the burnt house. "What are you going to do now?"

"I'm going to rebuild it," Bruce replied, "just the way it was."

The shadow of a bat was cast onto the clouds, ringed by a circle of light.

"Nice," said Batman, standing on the roof of the police station with Gordon. "What can I do for you, Sergeant?"

"It's Lieutenant now," Gordon replied. "You've started something. Hope on the streets . . . but we still haven't picked up Crane or half the inmates of Arkham that he freed." Gordon pulled out a clear evidence bag. "Take this guy," he said. "Got a taste for theatrics, like you. Leaves a calling card."

Inside the bag was a playing card — a joker. "I'll look into it," Batman said, and he stepped towards the edge of the roof, ready to leave.

"I never thanked you," Gordon called.

"You'll never have to," Batman replied.

He leapt off the rooftop and disappeared into the darkness.